Yoriko Tsutsui

ANNA IN CHARGE

illustrated by Akiko Hayashi

PUFFIN BOOKS

Anna was collecting pebbles from the path when her mother rushed out of the front door.

"Anna, I've got to go to the bank. I won't be long but if you need anything just ask Mrs Lee next door. She knows you're here by yourself. Now, don't go anywhere or speak to any strangers. I'll be back soon."

"But what about Katy?" Anna asked.

Her younger sister was inside.

"Katy is fast asleep. I'll be back before she wakes up."

Then Anna's mother dashed off.

A few moments later Anna
heard the sound of crying
coming from inside the house
– Katy had woken up!
Anna ran to open the front door
and there stood Katy in her
bare feet. She tried to go outside.
"Wait, Katy, I'll put your
shoes on. Then you can come
out to play!"
As soon as Katy had her shoes on
she stopped crying and ran outside.
"Hey, Katy! Wait for me!"
shouted Anna after her.

Katy wanted to see the pebbles
Anna had been collecting but
Anna had a better idea.
"No, don't go over there," she said
and took hold of Katy's hand. It
felt very small and soft and
suddenly Anna felt very tall and
grown-up.

Anna took a piece of chalk out of
her pocket and began to draw rail
tracks on the path.
"Katy, let's play choo-choo trains."
"Choo-choo, choo-choo!"
Katy laughed. She was having a
wonderful time! She ran down the
tracks which weren't quite
finished.
"No! Wait, Katy. Wait until I've
finished drawing them!"

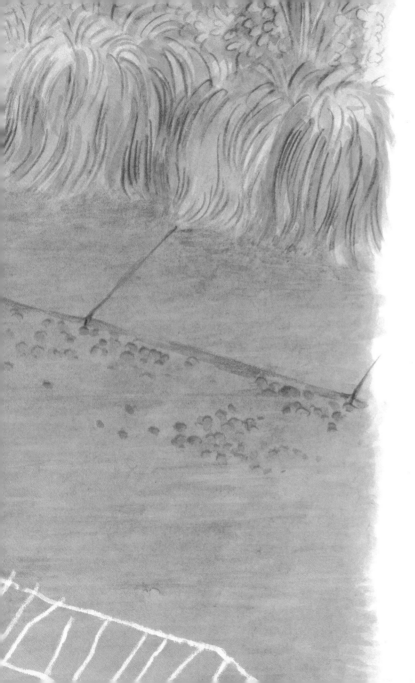

Katy stopped running and stood
still, waiting for the track to be
finished.
Anna wanted to draw the track
properly for Katy.
Anna drew and drew and drew.
"It's a long, long track, Katy, and
look, here's the station and I'll put
a mountain here ... and a tunnel!
All right, Katy, choo-choo, you can
go now. It's finished!"
Anna looked up.

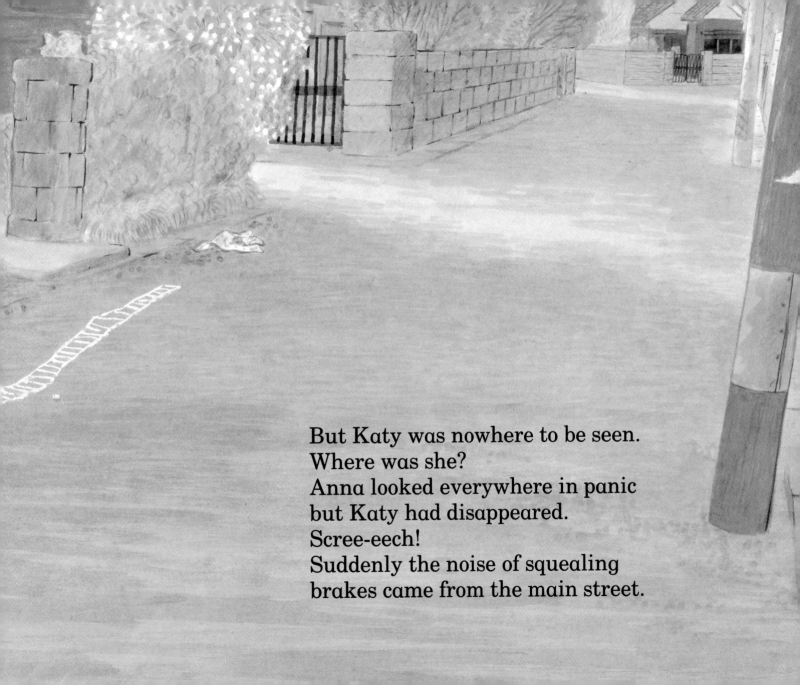

But Katy was nowhere to be seen.
Where was she?
Anna looked everywhere in panic
but Katy had disappeared.
Scree-eech!
Suddenly the noise of squealing
brakes came from the main street.

Anna ran in the direction of
the noise.
"Oh no! What if it's Katy!
What will I do if she's been hit
by a car!"
All she could hear was her
heart thumping with fear.

When she got to the main street
she heaved a sigh of relief.
It was only a bicycle that had
crashed into some boxes.
Katy was nowhere in sight.
But where was she?
"I know where Katy would go.
She'd go to play in the park."

Anna ran straight down the road towards the park where their mother always took Katy. Suddenly she spotted a little girl ahead of her.

"Katy!" Anna shouted.

But the little girl didn't even look round. She just kept on walking. Anna called out "Katy! Katy!" and ran after her.

Then the little girl looked round.
She was wearing the same clothes as Katy, but Anna had never seen this little girl before.

Anna kept on walking.
Suddenly she stopped.
She could hear a little girl crying.
The noise was coming from around
the corner.
It sounded just like Katy...

Then a man appeared. He was
holding a little girl's hand and she
was crying.
It wasn't Katy.
"Little girls who don't do as
they're told get into lots of
trouble," the man was telling the
little girl as they walked past.
Anna remembered what her
mother had told her before she
went out.
She was very worried.

It wasn't far to the park now.
Anna began to run.
"Katy! Katy!"
Her heart beat louder and
louder as she got closer to the
park.

At last she was at the park.
"Katy!"
There was Katy, playing in the sand!
This time there was no mistake.
It really was Katy!
She was safe!

Anna ran towards Katy.
When Katy spotted her she called
Anna's name and waved a sandy
hand at her sister.

Anna gave Katy a big hug.
"You gave me such a scare," she said.

PUFFIN BOOKS
Published by the Penguin Group
Viking Penguin, a division of Penguin Books USA Inc.,
375 Hudson Street, New York, New York 10014, U.S.A.
Penguin Books Ltd, 27 Wrights Lane, London W8 5TZ, England
Penguin Books Australia Ltd, Ringwood, Victoria, Australia
Penguin Books Canada Ltd, 2801 John Street, Markham, Ontario, Canada L3R 1B4
Penguin Books (N.Z.) Ltd, 182–190 Wairau Road, Auckland 10, New Zealand

Penguin Books Ltd, Registered Offices: Harmondsworth, Middlesex, England

First published in Great Britain by Penguin Books Ltd, 1988
First published in the United States of America by Viking Penguin Inc., 1989
Published in Picture Puffins, 1991
1 3 5 7 9 10 8 6 4 2
Text copyright © Yoriko Tsutsui, 1979
Illustrations copyright © Akiko Hayashi, 1979
All rights reserved

Original Japanese edition published in Fukuinkan Shoten, Tokyo, 1979.

LIBRARY OF CONGRESS CATALOGING IN PUBLICATION DATA
Tsutsui, Yoriko.   Anna in charge / by Yoriko Tsutsui ;
illustrated by Akiko Hayashi.   p.   cm.
Summary: Anna is left in charge of her little sister Katy, and
when Katy wanders off, Anna must use her wits to find her younger sister.
ISBN 0-14-050733-7
[1. Sisters—Fiction. 2. Lost children—Fiction.]   I. Hayashi,
Akiko, 1945-   ill. II. Title.
PZ7.T795A1 1991   [E]—dc20   90-42032

Printed in Hong Kong